Cinderella

As Told By

RUSSELL SHORTO

Illustrated By T. Lewis

Here is Cinderella's version of this famous story
Turn the book over and read the story from her sister's point of view

A BIRCH LANE PRESS BOOK

Published by Carol Publishing Group

Text Copyright © 1990 by Mowgli, Inc., and Russell Shorto
Illustration Copyright © 1990 by T. Lewis

A Birch Lane Press Book
Published by Carol Publishing Group

Editorial Offices
600 Madison Avenue
New York, NY 10022

Sales & Distribution Offices
120 Enterprise Avenue
Secaucus, NJ 07094

In Canada: Musson Book Company
A division of General Publishing Co. Limited
Don Mills, Ontario

Manufactured in the United States of America

10   9   8   7   6   5   4   3   2   1

Library of Congress Cataloging-in-Publication Data

Shorto, Russell.
Cinderella and Cinderella's stepsister / Russell Shorto;
illustrated by T. Lewis.
p.   cm.
Summary: After reading the classic tale of Cinderella, the reader
is invited to turn the book upside down and read an updated version
told from the "evil" stepsister's vantage point.
ISBN 1-55972-054-9 (cloth)
1. Toy and movable books—Specimens.   [1. Fairy tales.
2. Folklore.   3. Toy and movable books.]   I. Lewis, T. (Thomas),
ill.   II. Title.   III. Title: Cinderella's stepsister.
PZ8.S3445C1   1990
[398.2]—dc20
                                                    90-41900
                                                    CIP
                                                    AC

Once there was a girl who lived with her father in a beautiful cottage on the edge of the forest.

One day the father brought home a new wife, who had two daughters of her own. These girls had pretty faces but wicked hearts. They began ordering the man's daughter about like a servant.

The daughter worked day and night to please her stepsisters. Her nice clothes became rags. She was always covered with soot and cinders from cleaning the fireplace in the kitchen. The wicked stepsisters only made fun of her. "Look at her hair!" the older one said rudely. "It is full of cinders."

"So it is!" said the younger one. "Let's call her Cinderella!"

The two stepsisters laughed and laughed, and from that moment on they called the poor girl *Cinderella.*

One day word came that a great ball was to be held at the palace. The handsome prince would choose his bride at the ball. As Cinderella helped her stepsisters get ready, she asked, "What about me? Can't *I* come to the ball?"

The stepsisters could hardly believe their ears. "*You?*" they exclaimed. "You are so grubby and plain. Imagine the prince choosing you!" They laughed and laughed. Then they hopped into their carriage and were whisked off to the palace.

Cinderella watched the carriage disappear, tears streaming down her face. "I may be plain and grubby," she whispered, "but I would still like to go to the ball." She had forgotten that underneath the soot and cinders she was really a beautiful girl.

Suddenly a bright light appeared behind Cinderella. She turned around to find a strange woman with wings dressed in a long, silver cloak.

"I am your Fairy Godmother," the woman told Cinderella. "I have come to grant your wish. You are a good girl, and you deserve to go to the ball."

Cinderella dried her eyes. "But how can I?" she asked. "I have no coach. I have no horses. I have no fine gown."

"Tut tut!" the Fairy Godmother said, smiling. And, waving her magic wand, she turned a pumpkin into a beautiful gilded coach.

"Oh my! How wonderful!" cried Cinderella.

Then the Fairy Godmother spotted six mice scampering in the grass. With a wave of her wand they were changed into six horses.

Next she spied an old weasel sitting by the gate. She waved her wand again, and the weasel turned into a coachman—with the finest set of whiskers imaginable!

Then the Fairy Godmother turned to Cinderella and waved her wand a final time. Cinderella's tattered dress became a shimmering silver-blue ball gown, and her old wooden shoes turned into slender glass slippers.

"Oh, Fairy Godmother," Cinderella said softly, "how can I thank you?"

"Never mind me," the Fairy Godmother replied. "You just hurry to the ball. But remember one thing: at midnight everything will become as it was. So, my dear, you must leave the ball before the last stroke of twelve!"

And with that, the coachman opened the door and bowed. Cinderella stepped into the coach and was swept off to the ball.

At the palace, everyone asked the same question: "Who is that beautiful girl with the glass slippers?" Even Cinderella's stepsisters did not recognize her.

The prince was enchanted by her beauty, and the amazing stories she told him about mice and pumpkins. He danced with her all evening, and Cinderella had a wonderful time.

Suddenly she heard the clock begin to chime twelve. "Oh I'm sorry, Your Majesty," Cinderella cried, "but I must go!" And she ran down the steps and out of the palace.

She reached the gates just in time to watch her coach turn back into a pumpkin. Her horses became scampering mice again, and the coachman slithered away as a weasel. She looked down and saw that her beautiful gown was once more only a ragged old dress.

The prince ran outside, but he saw only a tearful girl in a tattered dress hurrying down the road. Then he spotted something on the steps. It was a slender glass slipper. The prince picked it up and gave it to his footman. "Search the kingdom for the owner of this slipper!" he commanded. "She is to be my bride!"

The prince's men searched high and low. They
went to every home and asked every young lady
to try on the slipper. But the slipper was too small
for all of them.

Finally the men came to Cinderella's house. The
elder stepsister eagerly took the slipper. Try as she
might, she could not get her foot into it. "Ouch!"

"Bring her here!" commanded the footman.

So Cinderella was called in from the kitchen, where she was busy scrubbing the floor. She sat down shyly, and stretched out her slender foot. The prince himself knelt and put the slipper on her foot.

Everyone gasped. *A perfect fit!*

The prince gazed into the girl's face and saw that she was indeed his true love. "My dear!" he cried.

"But I am only a poor, ragged girl with cinders in her hair," said Cinderella sadly.

"Nonsense!" the prince declared. "You are my beloved. We shall be married on Saturday."

And so poor Cinderella became the princess
of the kingdom, and nobody was so surprised as her
stepsisters at the way things turned out.

Cinderella and the prince lived happily ever
after, and that's the end of the story.

Or is it? Turn the book over . . . and we
shall see!

she finally cried. The younger stepsister snatched the slipper to try her luck. But it didn't fit her any better.

"Are there any other women in the house?" the prince's footman asked.

"There is only our grubby stepsister, Cinderella," answered the elder sister.